Temperament
Tales
A Journey of
Self-Discovery
For Children

To my children, who never stop revealing to me the
beauty of diversity in temperament.

What can there be?
What can I find? I Know...
Who am I?

Am I a Busy Bee,
pronouncing decrees, and
pursuing multiple degrees?

Like a flame that ignites,
the choleric shines bright,
leading with passion and
fiery might.

11 12 1
10 2
9 3
8 4
7 6 5

Or a bold, fun-loving, life-of-the-party basking in the sun? No need to fret if yellow is your choice. Sanguines help everyone rejoice!

With hearts so bright and spirits high, the sanguine brings joy as they touch the sky.

Perhaps thoughtfulness and creativity are more my jam...it takes all sorts to make the world go round!

The melancholic's heart is deep and true, a thoughtful soul with a shade of blue.

Maybe cool, calm, and collected is my thing. I just prefer the harmony that I bring. When I'm around, we all get along, because peace and friendship make me strong.

In tranquil waters they reside, the phlegmatic's calmness is their guide, steady and serene, their presence does peace provide.

Choleric
demanding
efficient
ambitious
intolerant
planner
too busy
leader
impatient
tense
confident
motivator
inflexible
Sanguine
impulsive
optimistic
often late
forgives
Sociable
out-going
forgetful
exaggerates
selfish
shameless
fun-loving
confident

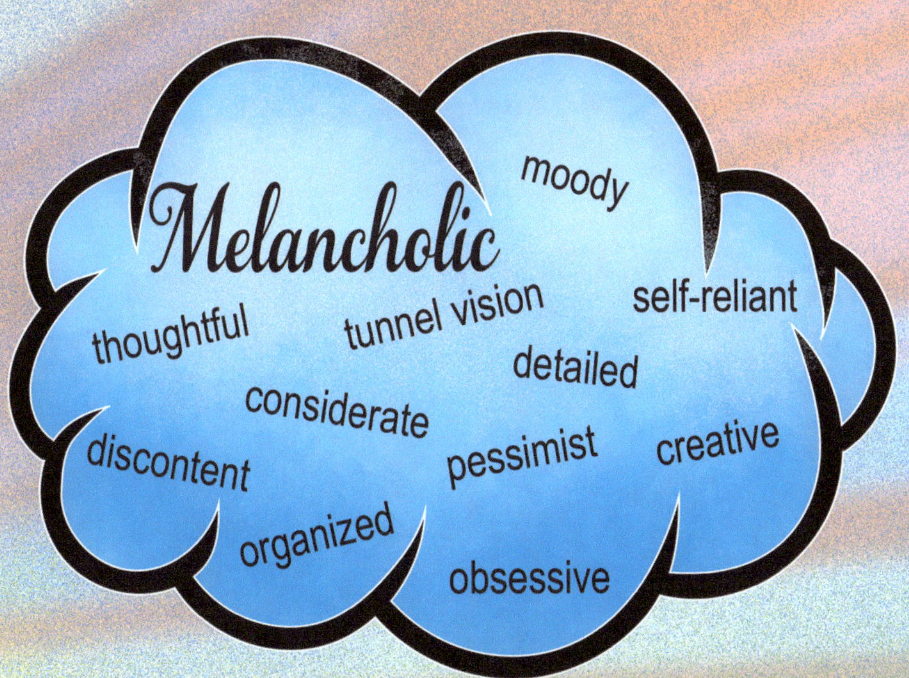

Melancholic
moody
thoughtful
tunnel vision
self-reliant
detailed
considerate
discontent
pessimist
creative
organized
obsessive

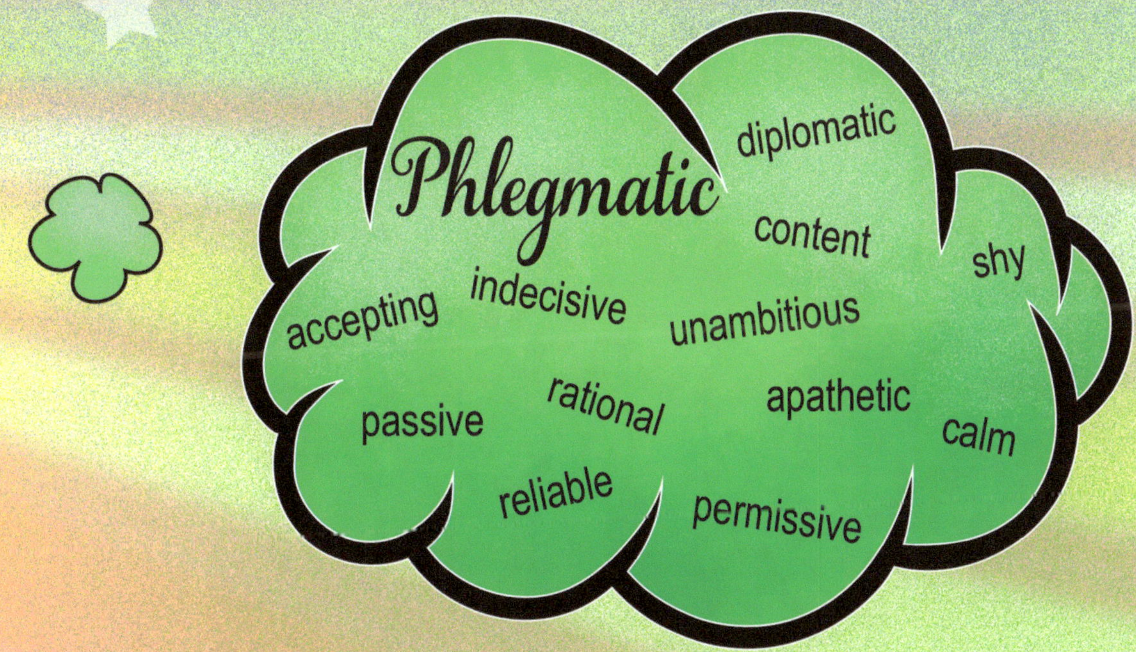

Phlegmatic
diplomatic
content
shy
accepting
indecisive
unambitious
passive
rational
apathetic
calm
reliable
permissive

Who am I? How can I know?

Talk to someone about the options below:

Questions to help identify your child's temperament:

What is my child's energy level?
How does my child react to new situations, people,
places, and things?
How readily can my child adapt to change or surprises?
Does my child depend on and form his/her own routine?
How does my child manage frustration?

**For further assistance, check out:
https://www.cdc.gov/childrensmentalhealth/index.html**

Please note, temperament is only a part of what will eventually form your child's identity. Aware of your child's temperament, their strengths can be utilized and nourished and their weaknesses attenuated. Lastly, never hesitate to reach out to trained professionals if you are concerned about your child's development or if you need support in any way to help your child thrive. You are the expert and know best!